# THE FOOLISH KING

Based on Hans Christian Andersen's "The Emperor's New Clothes"

E Wei

# by Lisl Weil

Macmillan Publishing Co., Inc., New York / Collier Macmillan Publishers, London

Macmillan Publishing Co., Inc.
866 Third Avenue, New York, N.Y. 10022
Collier Macmillan Canada, Inc.
Printed in the United States of America

10   9   8   7   6   5   4   3   2   1

*Library of Congress Cataloging in Publication Data*
Weil, Lisl.          The foolish king.
*Summary*: Mr. Humbug and Mr. Tricks, posing as tailors,
sell vain King Panache a suit of clothes which they
claim are invisible to anyone stupid.
[1. Fairy tales.  2. Kings, queens, rulers, etc.—Fiction]
I. Andersen, H. C. (Hans Christian), 1805-1875.
Kejserens nye klaeder.   II. Title.
PZ8.W429Fo 1982   [E]   82-4640   ISBN 0-02-792570-6

This is King Panache the Great.

All he cared about was being admired for his fancy clothe
And oh, what clothes he had! Dozens of pairs of shoes,
hundreds of suits, scores of hats and crowns, fabulous
outfits for every hour of the day for years to come.

But even so, King Panache wasn't satisfied.
He wanted something new, something special
to wear to the Grand Ball.

Should he dress up as a Chinese Great Ancestor?

Or what about a splendid Arab sheik?

Or a Scottish nobleman?

Nothing seemed just right and King Panache was very worried. But what luck! Just then the palace guards announced the arrival of two famous tailors.

Mr. Humbug and Mr. Tricks swept in. They bowed low. They smiled. "King Panache," they said, "your worries are over. We will make you a fantastic new costume, fashioned from a unique fabric woven on our special loom—a wonderful fabric that only clever people can see and appreciate, a fabric that is invisible to anyone stupid."

King Panache was intrigued and promised to pay the tailors handsomely for such a spectacular new outfit. With that, the tailors took the king's measurements—not once, but twice—then rushed off to set up the special loom.

Day and night, King Panache dreamed of his fantastic new clothes.

Day and night, the tailors
worked behind locked doors.
King Panache grew more and
more excited and more
and more curious. Finally,
he ordered his Prime Minister
and trusted counselors—the
cleverest men in his kingdom—
to check on the tailors'
progress.

The Prime Minister and trusted counselors looked and looked as the tailors showed them the loom and pointed out the fabric, its lovely colors and intricate design. The Prime Minister and trusted counselors nodded with admiration. None of them would admit that they could not see it. They didn't want to appear stupid, after all.

"Why, it is gorgeous!" the Prime Minister reported to the king. "Striking! Magnificent! Simply sublime!" And the trusted counselors agreed.

At last it was the day of the Grand Ball. And at last the
tailors delivered the king's new clothes.

"Here are your silvery silken trousers," they said as they
helped the king into them—sort of.

"Now for your purple
tufted tunic," they
said as they buttoned
it up—sort of.
"And finally, your
ruby red cape,"
they said as they
arranged the folds—
sort of.

"What a perfect fit!"
the tailors cried.

"What a disaster!"
thought King Panache.
"What dishonor! What
if my people find out
that *I* cannot see
my fine new clothes?"

"Very nice. Very nice indeed," he declared
and paid the tailors handsomely.

The royal trumpets sounded.
All eyes were on King Panache
as he strutted proudly into the
Grand Ball. Up and down the
ballroom he paraded and up and
down the ballroom he heard,

"What a charming outfit!"

"How handsome he looks!"

"It's fabulous! Ever so
beautiful!"

And then....

A young voice broke through the crowd, loud and clear. "But the king isn't wearing anything!"

For a moment there was silence.

And then....

Everyone roared
with laughter.
It was true!
King Panache wasn't
wearing anything.
The king was naked.
They couldn't stop
laughing at how the
tailors had fooled King
Panache the Great.

That is, until

They all realized
that they, too,
had been fooled
by the tricky
tailors.